Kadeer the Dreamer

Written by Kadeena Cox and Zoë Clarke
Illustrated by Jaleel Hudson

Collins

Prologue

The first thing I want to say is, this isn't a sad story. It's like I got on a bus, but instead of the bus taking its normal route, there was a bit of a detour. Quite a long detour, as it happens.

It turns out I was really on a mystery tour of my life. Things didn't turn out the way I thought they would, but I'm OK with that. I'm 18 now, but we're going back to when I was ten. You'll see why.

Chapter 1

I remember everything that happened on Tuesday 5th May.

It was a pretty normal day at school. In assembly, the Year Fours told us all about volcanoes, but when you're in Year Six, you know everything about them already, so I wasn't really paying attention. Mason in Year Five said his leg hurt and he had to be carried out of the hall by two teachers. He was definitely going to win the Attention Seeker of the Year award.

After assembly, my class teacher, Mrs Davis, gave us a surprise maths test. I can tell you now that no one likes surprises like this.

In the afternoon, it was creative writing, but my best mate, Isha and I were more interested in what the caretaker, Mr Coles, was doing. He'd leant a ladder against the mobile classroom and had clambered up it while holding a long broom. Then he began sweeping it across the roof to dislodge the balls the Year Fives had deliberately kicked up there. It was probably Mason, and that's why his leg hurt.

My favourite teachers, Ms Ashley and Mr Booth, were catching the balls as Mr Coles raked them off the roof, and putting them in a large net bag. They're the best people for that job as they take us for PE and they're used to running about.

5

It was Ms Ashley and Mr Booth who encouraged me to get into running. Once I started, I just kept going; I used to spend every lunchtime pelting around the playground, trying to complete circuits. I'd wake up every morning with jumpy legs; it sounds funny, but I needed to run like I needed to breathe.

I won every running race in PE, except the relay one time because Isha slipped in some mud and dropped the baton. On sports day, I was awarded a silver cup because I was so speedy.

The cup wasn't real silver, which was very disappointing; I'd made the effort to train, so I think the school could have made the effort and given me a solid silver cup. But no. I put it on the shelf above my desk at home, along with medals I'd won in other races. Every time I looked at the cup and the medals, I wondered what winning a *real* cup or medal would be like.

It was Ms Ashley who asked me if I'd heard of Leeds City Athletic Club. The club had an under-13s squad and she thought I might fit in there, so Mum took me along to see what it was all about. I didn't know there was somewhere I could go that just did sport – it was amazing! There were loads of kids from different schools in Leeds, and the indoor racing track was massive. When I saw the track and met the coaches, I knew that it was the place for me.

* * *

I'd been at the club a year now, training for the 100 metres and 200 metres sprint and I was looking forward to my training session that night.

I got home from school at quarter to four and filled my water bottle from the kitchen tap, ready to put in my kit bag. Someone had cut an article out of the paper and stuck it to the fridge. I knew it was meant for me because it was a list of 100 things to do before you're 12, and I was the only one in our house who was under 12. Mini and Max were only six, but they're dogs, and they can't read.

Some of the things on the list were quite interesting, like getting up early to see the sunrise and staying up late to go stargazing, but I was NOT going to go for a swim in the sea, and you'd NEVER see me ride a bike.

Mum used to say I might like to "broaden my horizons". I think she meant I should do lots of different activities, but there was only one activity I wanted to do, and that was RUN.

Coach Scobie at the athletic club said I had a "winning mindset"; I wanted to win so I made it happen. She was right; I *was* a winner.

I had a list of my own, but I'd never shown it to anyone. It was my secret Motivation List and there were three things on it: become a top athlete, represent my country at the Olympic Games and win an Olympic medal.

Chapter 2

"Kad! Can you hear me? If you don't get ready now, you'll be late!"

Mum and Dad should've named my older sister, Joy, "Shouty". The neighbours three doors down probably heard her.

"I packed my kit bag this morning before school," I remember yelling back. The neighbours probably heard that too.

I pulled on my tracksuit top and laced up my trainers. Mini and Max were sitting on the end of my bed. They wagged their tails and looked at me hopefully.

"I'll take you for a run when I get back," I promised them.

Joy is a very slow driver. Whenever I tell her to go faster, she just goes, "Mmm hmm" and continues to drive at ten miles an hour.

We somehow got to the athletic club, even with Joy's excruciating, sloth-like driving. I think it was about half past four. Joy used to sit trackside and half watch me and half read her latest "motivational and inspirational" book. She's my number one supporter; Mum and Dad are also my number one supporters (despite that list on the fridge). Then there's Grandad. He's my number one supporter, too.

"Life's better when you're laughing," Grandad always says. At breakfast, that morning he'd leant over and whispered, "Child, when you run, it's like you're laughing hard enough to make the whole world happy."

Jasmine said I couldn't have four number one supporters, but I didn't see why not. Jasmine was my best friend at the athletic club. We went to different schools at that point, but we'd joined the club at the same time. Sometimes she'd go quicker than me; sometimes I'd be quicker than her. We were both trying to beat Raya, but she'd been training for longer – she was supersonic!

We warmed up before racing began, and Jasmine and I improvised and made up dance routines once we were done. I think we could've been professional dancers.

I remember everyone taking their positions on the starting line for the 100 metres sprint.

Coach Scobie always told me to focus on my breathing. "That's the key, Kad. Regulate your breathing, make sure you get a strong push off and focus on the finish line."

I smiled at Jasmine. She smiled back and mouthed, "Winner, winner, chicken dinner."

The starting horn made me jump, and that'd never happened before. I stumbled out of the starting blocks and tried to regain my balance. I clenched my jaw, let my breath out and sprinted after Raya and Jasmine.

Focus, focus … focus, focus. I can hear the words echoing in my head, over and over, matching the rhythm of my feet on the track. I knew I was good; I knew I was fast; I knew I could beat Jasmine and Raya.

But the bad start meant I was several paces behind the others, and I blinked hard to stop tears of frustration forming as I watched Raya and Jasmine cross the finish line in front of me.

Coach Scobie wrote down our times. Mine was *not* going to go on the leader board.

"Are you OK, Kad?" Jasmine said, as she jogged over. "You kind of fell out of the starting blocks."

"Well, I think I got the breathing right, and I did focus on the finish line. That's two out of three." But two out of three wasn't good enough, I knew that.

I picked up my water bottle and glanced over at the trackside. Joy grinned at me. "Girl, you sure can run!" she always told me after each practice. This was usually followed by "You can run for the rest of us," because Joy does not do running.

Then everything happened in slow motion.

I looked at Jasmine and said, "I feel a bit funny."

And Jasmine replied, "Funny as in ha ha?"

I shook my head slowly. "You know when you lie in one position for too long and your arm or leg goes numb? It feels a bit like that." I felt a bit sick, too.

Then Jasmine said, "Your face looks strange, Kad, kind of lopsided. Lean on me."

But before I could do any leaning, I lost all feeling in my right leg and fell over, face first, flat on the track.

Chapter 3

"Kad! If you can hear me, squeeze my hand."

I *could* hear coach Scobie. She wasn't quite as loud as Joy, but loud enough. I remember I couldn't feel her hand, and I couldn't feel *my* hand either. Half my body felt heavy and numb, like I had bad pins and needles.

"I've called an ambulance." That was Joy. Her voice sounded a bit squeaky.

I was lying on the track, I couldn't feel my right-hand side and I had a banging pain above my right eye. I couldn't really see, so I must have hit my head quite hard.

I don't remember the ambulance arriving, the flashing lights, the siren, or being taken to hospital, but I had just fallen over and banged my head.

Joy told me later that she called Mum and Dad, drove home and collected them, and they raced to the hospital.

"Did you actually 'race to the hospital' or did you drive very slowly?" I asked her.

Joy gave me this wobbly smile, so I knew she'd probably driven a little bit faster than usual.

The next thing I remember was someone shining a very bright light in my eye.

A warm hand held mine and gave it a gentle squeeze. When I turned my head slowly to see who it was, I saw coach Scobie; she was holding my left hand, so I could feel it this time. I really wanted Mum and Dad.

"Kad?" she said. "It's going to be OK."

I could feel a tear forming in my left eye and coach Scobie held my hand tighter.

"Do you know where you are?" the doctor asked.

The words formed perfectly in my head, but I just couldn't translate them into speech. I meant to say Leeds General Hospital, but what came out was "Luffgol?" I tried again, but the words were trapped inside me.

The doctor made some notes and said, "When your parents get here, we'll have a chat about doing some tests to see why you fell over."

I'm not sure how long it was before Joy, Mum and Dad arrived, but I do know I cried. Well, I tried, but my whole face felt numb, and I ended up dribbling.

"Whatever this is," Mum said, "we'll find out what's going on." She looked quite fierce.

"I like that doctor," Dad said. He pulled the thin blanket up and tucked it around my shoulders; I wanted to tell him that meant my feet were sticking out at the other end, but I was scared the words wouldn't come.

Coach Scobie left and Joy played me a video of Top Ten Best Olympic Races, which she'd downloaded on her tablet. I think she'd read my secret Motivation List, though she didn't admit it then. We watched the videos together while Mum, Dad and the doctor had a chat. Mum was asking what was wrong with my speech, but I couldn't hear the reply.

"They're going to keep you in overnight," Mum said, when they'd finished talking about me.

Dad nodded. "The doctor wants you to have a brain scan in the morning."

They can scan your brain? I remember thinking. I didn't know what a brain scan was, or why I needed one. I was really tired.

"We'll be back tomorrow morning," Dad said. He put his hand in his jacket pocket and pulled out one of my medals and folded my left hand around it.

The hospital bed had scratchy sheets, and they were tightly tucked in, so it was hard to move. It was odd without Mini and Max at the end of the bed making snuffling noises. I hoped Joy would smuggle them in to see me.

I remember replaying the day over and over in my head. Was it something I'd done, or not done? Maybe if I'd eaten more at lunch or warmed up differently, I might not have fallen over.

When I finally fell asleep, I dreamed I was running, but I just couldn't reach the finish line.

Mum and Dad were back the next morning. Mum should have been teaching food tech at Wetherby High School, but she said she'd taken time off. Dad's a projectionist at the Cottage Road Cinema – he makes sure the right films get shown at the right time – but he works in the evening.

There was a new doctor. She introduced herself as Doctor Orton, and she told me what was going to happen next. "I'm going to send you for a CT scan. The scanner looks a bit like a doughnut. You'll be placed on a special bed that moves through the centre of the doughnut and the machine will scan your body and take pictures of your brain. The images should tell us what happened to you yesterday."

I concentrated on what I wanted to say, formed the words, and breathed out "OK". I could talk properly – sort of! I also wanted to eat a doughnut.

Doctor Orton smiled. "You'll have to lie very still, and we'll give you some headphones so you can hear music while the machine is working."

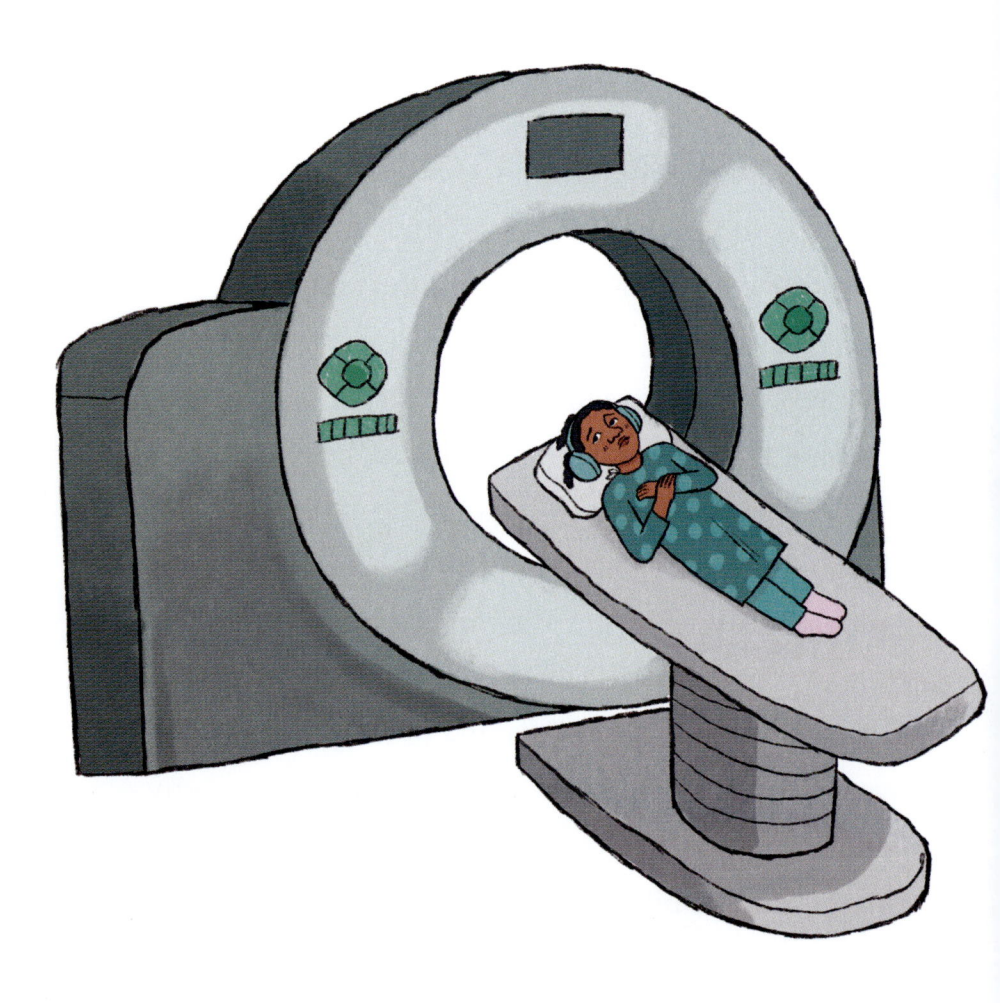

Doctor Orton was right; the machine did look like a doughnut. As the music played through the headphones, I pretended that each beat was the sound of my running shoes on the track as I sprinted for the finish line.

After I had my scan, I slept for a bit. I woke up when I heard a trolley clattering into the ward with lunch. I looked at the limp cheese and pickle sandwich I'd been given, squeezed my eyes tight and thought about home.

Mum and Dad were back after lunch, and Joy was with them. She hadn't smuggled Mini and Max in. Then I remembered. "Mini and Max! I never took them for their run after training." The words came out in a jumble, but I definitely had my speaking mojo back! I just hoped I wasn't dribbling again.

"I took them out," Joy told me.

I looked at her. "Did you, really? Did you actually run?"

Joy pulled a face. "I did a walk-jog. They've only got little legs."

She had a point. Mini and Max do only have little legs.

Doctor Orton had news. She pulled the curtains around my bed "for privacy", but they weren't noise cancelling curtains, so there wasn't much point.

"I've had a look at the scans we took of your brain this morning," Doctor Orton said. "They show that yesterday Kad suffered what we call a childhood stroke."

Mum made a noise that sounded like a cross between a gasp and a sob. I could see Dad pressing Mum's hand. Joy usually had something to say about everything, but she'd suddenly gone very quiet.

"What's a childhood stroke?" I asked.

"About one in 400 young people up to the age of 18 can suffer a childhood stroke. It's when the blood supply to part of your brain is cut off," Doctor Orton replied. "That's what caused your right side to go numb, though I'm pleased to see your speech has come back."

"Why me, though?" I asked.

Doctor Orton shook her head. "We don't always know why strokes happen; we might need to do some more investigating."

"Like a detective," I said. "A brain detective."

"No one's called me a brain detective before," Doctor Orton said, "but I like it." She looked at Mum and Dad, and then turned back to me. "The good news is, because you were admitted to hospital so quickly, we were able to help you immediately. You'll need to take some medication and you're going to feel quite tired. You might not feel like doing some of the things you used to, but you'll start to feel better, and we'll monitor your progress."

"I still want to run," I said. "I can still run, can't I?"

Chapter 4

I wasn't allowed to run.

I was in hospital for three weeks, and the only good thing about that was I missed the times tables test. Mrs Davis sent me the biggest get-well card I'd ever seen, which everyone in my class had signed. Isha's signature took up most of the inside. Ms Ashley and Mr Booth sent me a card with a runner on it, and coach Scobie came in to see me.

"Think about what I taught you, Kad," she said. "Focus on the finish line and you'll get there."

I realise now that she wasn't talking about running.

Jasmine visited with her mum and told me I had to get better because there was an athletics competition coming up. She bought me a magazine about running. When they'd gone, I looked at the cover, but I didn't feel like reading it. The stories were supposed to inspire people, but I felt angry before I'd even opened it. I think I was angry with Jasmine too because she could still run when I couldn't.

I told Mum about the cheese and pickle sandwiches, and she wrinkled her nose. Mum makes the best brown stew chicken, and Dad's Friday night curried lamb is legendary, according to him. Even Grandad has what he calls his "signature dish", which is rice and peas.

That's when Mum started bringing in food in plastic lunchboxes.

I made a "skwee" sound the first time she handed a box over. I popped the lid open, and the smell of jerk chicken wafted towards me; it made me forget where I was and why I was there – just for a moment.

I didn't have any more pins and needles in my arm and leg, but my feet were feeling jumpy 'cos they just wanted to move, so it was a great day when Doctor Orton said I could go home to finish recuperating. That's just a fancy word for "recovering". I really did think that was it – recuperation and then back to how things had been before.

Joy drove me, Dad and Mum home. I didn't mind her being slow – I leant my head against the cool window and stared at the outside world like it was the first time I'd ever seen a row of houses, or a tree. I could see out of the window when I was in hospital, but it wasn't the same.

Grandad was waiting for us when we got home. He was holding Mini in one arm, and Max in the other. He also had a party hat on, even though it wasn't my birthday, which made me smile.

"You keep laughing, child," Grandad said.

So that was the first thing that happened to me. I had a stroke and then I felt better. That's not the end of the story though. The second thing that happened made me realise my life was going to change forever. But it's like I said, this isn't a sad story.

By the time I returned to school it was mid-June. The Year Fours had moved on to Romans and performed a dramatic sword fight in assembly. Mason was complaining about his arm this time, but he didn't get carried out. Mrs Davis was still setting times tables tests, and Mr Coles was still raking footballs off the mobile classroom roof. Ms Ashley and Mr Booth saw me looking out of the window and gave me a wave.

Doctor Orton said I could start some light exercise, but I had to take it slowly. When I was in hospital, I had to walk on a treadmill on low speed.

"Every step feels like I'm wading through mud," I'd complained to the physiotherapist who was looking after me. But I gritted my teeth and focused on an imaginary finish line.

There was a stationary bike, too. I know I said I wasn't ever going to get on a bicycle, but I gave it a go. If you switch the gear to the lowest, it's almost like the bike is doing all the work.

Then it clicked in my brain: I leant forward slightly, tucked my head in and pressed down on the pedals. I remember closing my eyes, and for a moment, the movement felt almost as freeing as running – like I could ride that bike straight off the stand and out of the hospital.

I remember the physiotherapist standing back and folding his arms as he watched me cycle. "Nice technique," he said.

Even a few weeks after I got out of hospital, I still got tired just walking Mini and Max round the park, so I knew Doctor Orton was right about taking it slow. *I'd be faster on a bike*, I remember thinking.

Mrs Davis always encouraged everyone to expand their vocabulary when writing descriptions. My new word to describe how I felt when I saw people running in the park and all I wanted to do was join them was this: wistful.

33

"You've got to keep your brain active, even if your feet aren't active," Grandad told me.

"Grandad, are you trying to cheer me up?" I asked.

"Yes. Is it working?" he replied.

I shrugged. "Not really. Sorry."

He challenged me to dominoes every afternoon after school, but he always made up the rules as he went along.

Someone had taken down the list of 100 things to do, but I found it in a pile of magazines in the living room and put it back on the fridge. I thought about doing some of the 100 things while I was waiting for life to get back to normal. I ticked "Go for a bike ride". All that cycling in hospital surely had to count for something.

It was mid-July, and the day before I was going to return to the athletic club. I'd told Jasmine I'd be there, so I went to my room to get my tracksuit and running shoes. I walked over to my kit bag, but my legs wouldn't do what I wanted them to, and it felt like I was leaning over to one side. I could feel my right arm start to shake and then it felt like I had pins and needles.

I sunk down to the floor and said, "Not a stroke," over and over. Doctor Orton had told Mum, Dad and Joy to look out for the signs, just in case it happened again. I know Mum gave Grandad a list of symptoms, because I'd heard him recite them when he thought I wasn't listening.

I closed my eyes tight and curled up in a ball.

After a bit, I opened one eye, then the other. My arm had stopped shaking, there were no pins and needles and I felt OK. I remember letting out a shaky breath. "What do you think of that?" I said to Mini and Max. They'd curled up beside me while I'd been on the floor. "Not a stroke."

I stood up, took a first step and then another. I went over to my desk and held on to the edge tightly. My Motivation List was in the desk drawer, and I pulled it out and put it underneath my pillow, for luck.

I grabbed my kit bag and stomped downstairs (just to prove I could still stomp) and dropped it by the front door. *I AM going running tomorrow*, I promised myself.

But it's not always possible to keep promises, however much you mean them.

Chapter 5

The next day it felt like I was walking through the doors of the althletic club for the first time. Only this time Jasmine and coach Scobie started clapping, and then everyone joined in. Coach Scobie took a photograph of us all. The picture's still up on the club website and I look back at it sometimes.

"I could get used to this," I said.

Jasmine grinned and gave me a hug. "I knew you'd be back! I told my gran about you, and she said, 'Life's hurdles are there to be jumped over'."

"That sounds like something my grandad would say," I replied. "I don't think I'm going to jump any actual hurdles today."

A couple of my classmates didn't think anything had happened to me because I "looked the same" as before. How was I supposed to look, green with horns? I didn't feel quite the same inside, but no one could see that.

Coach Scobie got us to warm up, and then I was going to do some jogs, while the others started racing, just to get my running legs back. Joy gave me a massive grin from the trackside.

It was during the warm-up that I realised my running legs weren't coming back. My balance felt off, like it had the night before in my room. I walked slowly over to Joy.

"I don't think I can run," I said. "I can't even jog." I was trying really hard not to cry.

Joy grasped my shoulders. "You will run, Kad, but maybe not today. You need to learn to rest, not quit."

I sniffed. "That's why you're my number one supporter. You make me believe anything's possible."

We had a long hug, and Joy laughed. "Of *course* I'm your number one supporter – along with Mum, Dad and Grandad!"

I wrote that at the bottom of my Motivation List, so she's definitely been snooping in my room. I told coach Scobie and Jasmine that I'd be back the following week, but as we walked to Joy's car my balance went again, and I couldn't even walk in a straight line.

When we got home, I was in trouble with Mum and Dad.

"Why?" Mum kept asking. "Why didn't you tell us about what happened in your room?"

"We need to be able to help you, Kad," Dad said. "And we can't do that if you don't tell us when you're not feeling well."

"It didn't feel the same as before, and then I felt OK afterwards, so I thought everything was fine," I said.

"And you wanted to go back to the althletic club," Mum said.

"Yes!" I shouted. "I wanted to go to the athletic club. I wanted to run. I *want* to run!"

There was a bit of a silence. Then Grandad said, "Child, these setbacks are just temporary. They'll help you see your true strengths."

I really did cry then. Big, ugly sobs of rage and frustration. "But I can't run! I can't even *walk* straight."

Joy handed me a box of tissues, and Mini and Max, who'd been hiding under the sofa, came out and jumped onto my lap.

The next day we were back at Leeds General Hospital. There were more tests the doctors said they wanted to do, to see if there was anything else going on with my balance. Doctor Orton gave me a big smile when she saw me. She told me I hadn't had another stroke. I could have told her that. Actually, I *did* tell her that, but I suppose she needed to make sure, so I had to go through the doughnut-shaped brain scanner again.

This time there was a new doctor. "Doctor Khan is a neurologist," Doctor Orton said. "Neurologists look at things like the brain, spinal cord, nerves or muscles."

Doctor Khan looked at my eyes to see if my sight had changed. Then sticky patches were placed on my head, and I had to look at light patterns on a screen.

I had to stay in hospital for a few days, but it was easier this time as I knew what to expect, like cheese and pickle sandwiches. Joy didn't smuggle Mini and Max in, but she did make a video of them wearing silly knitted coats.

The next morning, the curtains were pulled round my bed again, which meant Doctor Khan had something important to say. Mum and Dad were trying not to look worried, but I could see they were.

"We can't give a firm diagnosis from these two episodes you've had," Doctor Khan said. "But we believe you're showing symptoms that may develop into multiple sclerosis. We sometimes call that MS, for short. Monitoring you over time will help us accurately diagnose your condition."

"Is that different from a stroke?" I asked.

Doctor Khan nodded. "It is, yes."

I was going to ask about whether I could run, but I was afraid I wouldn't like the answer, so I kept quiet.

If those two "episodes" weren't enough for Doctor Orton and Doctor Khan to diagnose me, by the time I'd had four more, they said they were confident I had multiple sclerosis. The only thing they didn't know was what type I had. This would take years to find out.

I looked it up on Mum's laptop and learnt that there were different types. I even made notes. Some people with MS get better and then worse, then better, then worse. Others get slowly worse over time. There wasn't a third type, where you just got better and stayed better.

I found out so much that if I'd taken a GCSE in multiple sclerosis, I think I might've got Grade 9. But the more I found out, the more I realised that I wasn't going to make it to the Olympics after all. I shoved my sports kit and running shoes under my bed, as far as they would go. Then I screwed up my Motivation List and threw it in the corner of my room.

So that's the second thing that happened to me. I had a stroke and then I was diagnosed with multiple sclerosis.

I felt angry quite a lot of the time, but then something Grandad said made me look at things differently. We were playing dominoes and he'd just made up a rule that meant he could match any two pieces together. Then he said, just out of the blue, "The journey isn't the same for everyone."

I thought about that long and hard: while I was taking Mini and Max (and Joy) for a slow walk, while I was helping Dad cook dinner, while I watched Jasmine win a medal at a local athletics competition.

The last time I made a promise to myself it didn't work, but that wasn't a good enough reason not to make another one. I promised myself that I wasn't going to let what was happening to me change what I wanted to do.

I went up to my room and retrieved the crumpled Motivation List. I flattened it out and stared at the points long and hard. I was going to find a *different* way of making my dreams come true. I just didn't know how.

Chapter 6

I'd missed the end of school; it was the summer holiday. No end of year party for me, no writing on everyone's school shirts, no water fight with the teachers on the last day. So that's what I didn't do, and that left … what? Time to stare at my bedroom wall, trying to work out how to motivate myself.

After about a week, Mum said, "I'm not having this. I'm not having you stare at your bedroom wall trying to work out how to motivate yourself." It was like she'd read my mind. "I chatted to Doctor Khan, and she suggested you might benefit from going to the seaside."

"Isn't that what they used to do in Victorian times?" I asked. "You know, take the ill family member to the seaside for some bracing sea air." Mum looked a bit guilty when I said that, so I let her off. "It's OK. I *am* the ill family member, and I'd like to go to the seaside."

I wasn't sure how we were all going to fit in Joy's tiny car, though.

Mum hired a car! There was enough room for Mum, Dad, Grandad, me, Mini and Max. There was a lot of luggage to fit in too. Joy said she'd drive there slowly a couple of days later. Mum had picked Whitby, somewhere we hadn't been since I was about five.

"We used to swim in the sea all the time there," Joy said, but I didn't remember that. I remember thinking I could tick the swimming challenge off the list of 100 things – I noticed that someone had tucked the list in the pocket of the car seat before we left.

WHITBY
NORTH RIDING FOREST PARK
PICKERING
MALTON
YORK
STAMFORD BRIDGE
HOLTBY
LEEDS

I knew the first bit, from Leeds to York.

Dad pretended to be a tourist guide.

"York! Invaded by the Normans, and the Vikings … and tourists!

"If you look to your left, you'll see York is a fine example of a walled city!

"Voted one of the most haunted places in Europe!"

I'd never seen any ghosts there.

I remember saying to myself: "By Holtby, you'll have come up with a motivation plan". Then: "By Stamford Bridge Road, you'll have come up with a motivation plan". But Holtby and Stamford Bridge came and went, then Malton, then Pickering, and I'd come up empty.

I almost didn't want to go any further, but then we got to the North York Moors. There was miles and miles of open space: no buildings, no noise, nothing. It was strange but it made me forget about everything else. That was until Dad started saying things like, "Hippo on the left!" In case you've never been to North Riding Forest Park, there are exactly zero hippos.

I put my earphones in, closed my eyes and dreamed of green things.

The thing about Whitby that's different from Leeds is the bright, clear light. I think the sun reflects off the sea, or something. There was also the salty smell and taste. And the dive-bombing seagulls. The main thing, though, is Dracula. I wasn't supposed to be telling a spooky story, but we *were* staying in an area of outstanding natural spookiness, so that's probably why things got a bit weird.

The man who wrote *Dracula,* in eighteen something or other, visited Whitby, had a wander around the abbey, went to a local library at the end of the quay, and was inspired to call his vampire Dracula after something he read in a book there. I knew this because I looked up Whitby on the laptop after Mum told me about her seaside plans. Apparently, people scare themselves silly by wandering around the abbey late at night looking for the actual Dracula.

There are exactly 199 steps up to the abbey. I'd no intention of looking for Dracula, but I knew I probably couldn't climb all those steps even if I wanted to. The problem was, just thinking that I couldn't do something made me want to do it more; my brain was running ahead, but my legs weren't. Then I had an idea: I could walk up maybe 20 steps one day, and then down again, then try 30 steps the day after, and down again.

I drew a chart so I could track how many steps I walked up each day. When I explained to Grandad what I was doing, he said, "That's right, child. Don't ever be defined by your circumstances." He then whispered that there was a car park near the abbey, so if I wanted a day off, Mum or Dad could drive us up and we could look at the view without climbing the steps. It wouldn't be cheating, he said, as we'd still try to walk each day.

I was going to help Mum and Dad unpack the car, but Grandad pulled out a Spooky Map of Whitby and asked me to pick somewhere interesting. When I look back on it, I think Grandad was supposed to distract me, but when he went to find his glasses, I looked out of the window and saw Mum and Dad wrestling with an object from the back of the car. It was a wheelchair.

Chapter 7

I'd done enough MS investigating to know that I might need a walking stick or a wheelchair at some point; Mum and Dad had gone straight for the wheelchair option. This is how I knew I'd never fulfil my original Motivation List. I couldn't really compete against top athletes if I was using a wheelchair, could I?

"It's just in case," Dad said, when I confronted them. They couldn't really hide the fact they were trying to angle the thing through the narrow hallway.

"Just in case what?" I replied.

"Just in case you lose your balance again," Mum told me. "It would mean we can still go out and about."

"Well, you can see I have two perfectly good working legs," I said, doing a slow jog on the spot. "So, I *won't* be needing that."

Later that night, I looked out of the window at the lights in the harbour. "A good idea would be fantastic right about now," I told myself.

The following morning, I went out early with Grandad, before Mum and Dad were up, and took Mini and Max for a quick walk. Grandad always woke up early; he said it was his age. I'd been waking up early too, but that was for a different reason. I always wondered if I would have a good day or a bad day.

It turned out to be a good day. As we stood at the bottom of the Whitby Abbey steps, Grandad said, "Race you to the top!"

We both started laughing and counted the steps as we climbed. Did we get to 199? No, not even close. But it was a start.

By the time Joy joined us, we'd got to 30. "Girl, you sure can do steps," she said, looking at my chart.

But then I didn't have a good day. My legs wouldn't do what I wanted them to, and Joy found me on the bedroom floor after I'd tried to get out of bed and my legs refused to hold me upright.

"It's not fair!" I cried into Joy's shoulder. "I did 30 steps yesterday and today nothing!"

Joy held me tight. "Why don't we take my little car and drive up to the abbey instead?"

She helped me get dressed and down to her car. Grandad was right. There was a car park near the abbey.

We sat on a bench and looked down over Whitby and the sea beyond. "Mum and Dad brought a wheelchair," I told Joy.

"Yes, I know," she said.

"I'm not using it," I replied.

"All right, Miss Stubborn," Joy huffed.

As the sun rose, I said, "I can tick that one off the list of 100 things – get up early and watch the sun rise."

"That's my girl," Joy smiled.

59

The following day was better, but I didn't try climbing the steps.

"Why don't we see how those legs do in water?" Mum suggested.

"Beach day!" Joy said.

So that's how I found myself in the sea. It was a bit cold, but Joy held one of my hands, and Dad held the other, and we jumped up and down as the waves came in.

"I think my legs do well in water," I told Mum.

"Mmm-hmm," she replied.

"Are you trying to get me to tick off everything on that list you put on the fridge?" I asked.

Mum looked at me. "I didn't put the list on the fridge."

"Don't look at me!" Dad said. "But it was a good list."

I looked at Grandad and Joy, trying to work out who had the guiltiest face. "Joy!" I said, and flicked sand at her. "I thought you were my number one supporter!"

"I *am*," she protested. "But I accidentally read your secret Motivation List and I thought you could try and do some easier things first."

"Oh, you *accidentally* read it," I said. "I knew it!"

"Girl, you're not very good at hiding things," Joy replied.

"What list is this now?" Dad asked.

I made a face at Joy. "My Motivation List. I wrote down all the things I wanted to do, but now I'll never get to do them!" But I didn't feel quite as sad as I'd been before.

Mum, Dad and Grandad listened while I told them what was on the list.

"Oh, Kad," Mum said. "I'm sorry."

"I know ice cream won't solve this, but I think we need some," Dad said. "And Joy, you're going to go and get them."

61

If you're waiting for the spooky bit, this is it.

I was quite tired after the beach and went to bed early. Then a huge storm hit Whitby that night, and rain battered my bedroom window, and woke me up.

I sat up in bed and stared at the rain through a crack in the curtains. That's when the blank wall at the end of my bed suddenly lit up. An image appeared on the wall, like a home cinema, and I wondered if Dad had set up a projector, like the ones he uses at the Cottage Road Cinema.

I saw cyclists racing round and round a steep track. It looked like they were racing against each other, and also against a clock, as there were numbers counting up in the corner of the image. After three laps, the racers crossed the finish line and the clock stopped.

I rubbed my eyes. Doctor Khan said my eyesight might change, but I didn't think seeing cyclists was what she meant.

Then one of the cyclists dismounted and stretched out their hand towards mine. I stood up on the bed, making sure I didn't tread on Mini and Max, and walked straight into the image.

Chapter 8

The roar of the crowd was so loud! I was in the image I'd seen projected on the wall, standing trackside. The cyclist who'd invited me in was now on the track. There were two people holding on to the back of their bicycle, and then four loud beeps sounded … and the cyclist was off!

A clock on a big screen counted the seconds the cyclist took, as they raced round the track. The crowd got louder and louder. An official rang the bell, and the last lap went by in a flash!

Then the image imploded, and the light went off, as if it had never been there in the first place. I was back in bed, looking at the blank wall and listening to the rain outside. Snuffles came from the end of the bed, where Mini and Max were still asleep.

Just before the image dissolved, the cyclist had removed their helmet and visor and I saw … it was me.

67

The next morning, I had questions. "Joy, have you ever seen things?"

Joy looked at me. "You're going to have to be a bit more specific."

"Visions. Like visions of the future," I said.

"That sounds a bit Dickensian," Joy replied.

"I don't know what that is," I said. Sometimes Joy talks like the books she reads.

Joy sighed. "Charles Dickens. He wrote a book where a mean old man is visited by four ghosts, and one of the ghosts shows him what his future is going to be like."

"Muppets!" Grandad said.

Joy sighed. "Yes, the book has been made into a film several times, and the best version has the Muppets in it."

"Have you had a vision, Kad?" Joy asked.

"I think I might have," I said. "But there weren't any ghosts because they don't exist. A bit like Dracula."

"Don't say that around here!" Dad said from the hallway. He was manoeuvring the wheelchair back into the car, as this was our last day in Whitby, and I was *not* going to need it.

Joy put down her piece of toast. "Come on, out with it. What's this vision you saw?"

"Well, it was me, in the future. And I was on a bicycle."

"That physiotherapist at Leeds General did say you had a nice technique when you were on the stationary bike," Dad reminded me.

"So, I was wondering if there was some kind of bike racing I could do now that I've got MS," I said. "Like the Olympics, but for me."

"Well, of course there is," Joy said. She opened her tablet and showed me. "The Paralympics."

Chapter 9

August rolled into September, and I started secondary school. I was at Wetherby High School where Mum taught. Some things were different, like I had to use a walking stick or wheelchair when my legs just didn't want to work. Some things were the same, like me and Isha watching the caretaker retrieve footballs from the roof. Jasmine joined the school too, so that was two of my favourite people in the same class with me.

I'd done lots of research on the Paralympics (my next best subject after multiple sclerosis) so when I went back to the althletic club to see coach Scobie, and she suggested working with some specialist coaches, I knew what she was talking about.

"These coaches work with athletes who show potential to represent the country at the Paralympics," she said.

So, I started training with coach Rees. I worked my way back up to running the 100 and 200 metres, just like I had before I was diagnosed, and I got on a bike! I also learned about athletes who competed using a wheelchair – suddenly the wheelchair wasn't as bad as I'd thought.

I trained twice a week, and then I did other stuff in between. This is what my week looked like after school.

Monday	Tuesday	Wednesday	Thursday	Friday
swimming	training at the club	swimming	training at the club	swimming
	warm-up		warm-up	
	weights		weights	
	treadmill/ running		cycling	

Weightlifting built up my muscles and helped me stay fit. Doctor Khan said that keeping fit meant I could achieve my goals. I also had to eat lots of good food. Mum, Dad and Grandad's cooking was still the best, and Joy made me a sandwich now and then, just not cheese and pickle.

73

My new and improved Motivation List looked like this:
Become a top athlete
Represent my country at the Paralympic Games
Win a Paralympic medal

So, what you might be wondering is: what happened next? Did she burn up that treadmill, lift all those weights, and could she ride that stationary bike right out of the hospital?

Oh yes! I was picked to represent Great Britain at the Paralympics: 100 metres, 200 metres, 400 metres, paracycling … I've won Bronze medals, Silver medals and best of all – GOLD. The Silver and Gold medals are at least 92.5% *real* silver and gold!

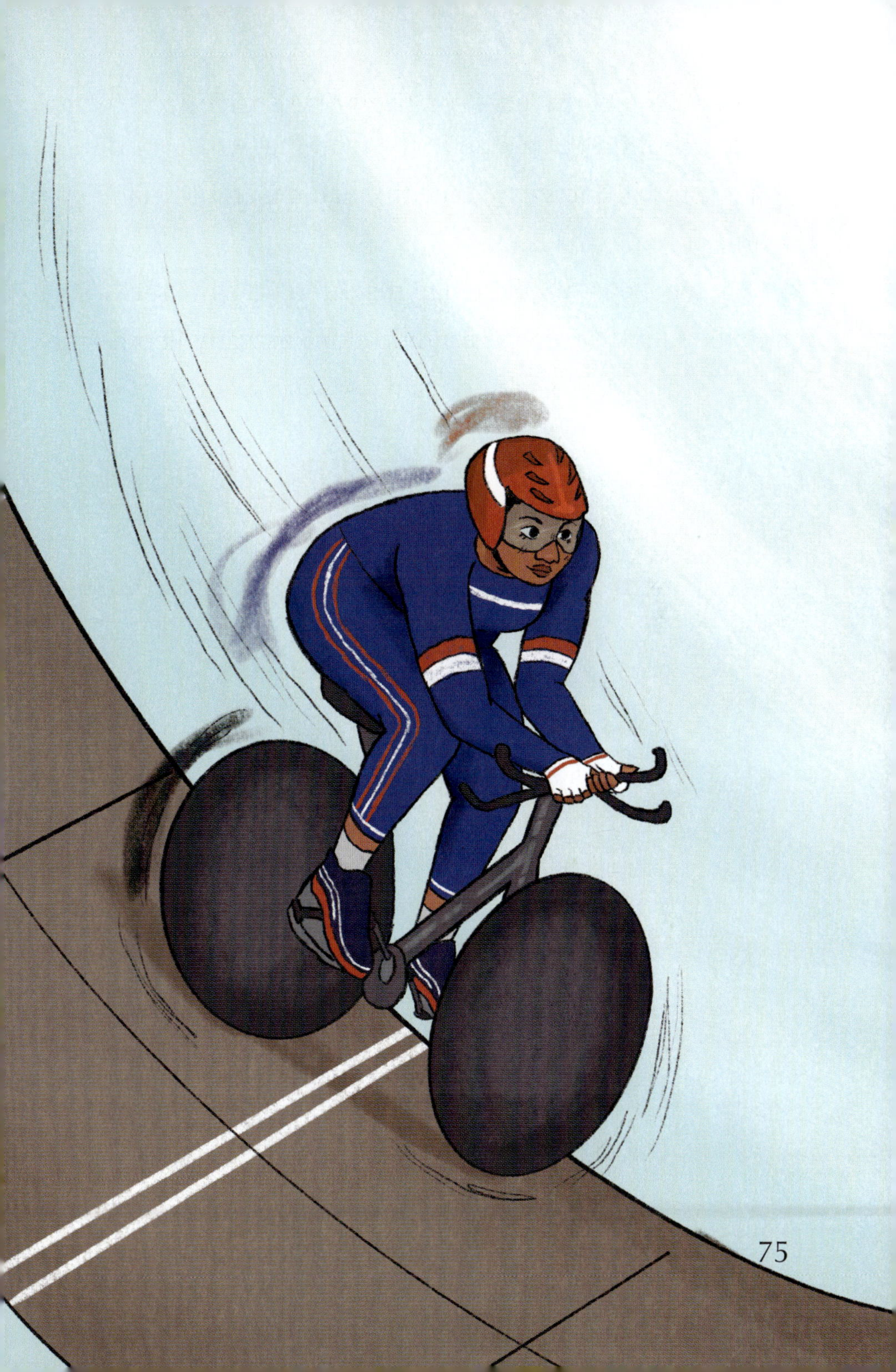

Running and cycling gave me hope when I didn't think I had any. Sport got me up in the morning, whatever my body felt like, and carried me through the day. My family and friends did that too.

So that's what happened to me. All of it. Did I really step into the future or did I dream it? I don't actually know.

I'm still on a journey, and I'm going to do something that's bigger than me. I'm going to make history.

I'm still working through that list on the fridge, even though I'm older than 12. In fact, Joy's laid out a blanket in the garden and we're going to stay up late and stargaze.

This is not a sad story.

MY LIFE IN PICTURES

78

79

Ideas for reading

Written by Christine Whitney
Primary Literacy Consultant

Reading objectives:
- check that the text makes sense, discuss their understanding and explore the meaning of words in context
- draw inferences such as inferring characters' feelings, thoughts and motives from their actions
- predict what might happen from details stated and implied
- identify main ideas drawn from more than one paragraph and summarise these
- identify and discuss themes in a wide range of writing
- provide reasoned justifications for their views

Spoken language objectives:
- participate in discussion
- speculate, hypothesise, imagine and explore ideas through talk
- ask relevant questions

Curriculum links: PSHE education: learn to recognise the ways in which they are the same and different to others

Interest words: motivation, diagnose, physiotherapist, circumstances, multiple sclerosis

Build a context for reading
- Before looking at the book, encourage children to discuss what they would like to achieve in their life. What are their hopes for the future?
- Look at the illustration on the front cover. Ask children to predict what Kadeena dreams of becoming.
- Read the blurb on the back cover. Encourage the group to discuss what additional information is given here and what it might mean for the story.

Understand and apply reading strategies
- Read Chapter 1 together. Summarise what the reader knows about Kadeena by the end of the chapter.
- Continue to read together up to the end of Chapter 2. Ask children to describe the problems Kadeena faced at her athletics meeting. How does the chapter end?
- Read Chapter 3 together. Support children as they describe step-by-step the medical tests Kadeena underwent. What diagnosis was made at the end of the chapter?
- Read Chapter 4. Ask children to explain what Kadeena meant on p29 when she said, *The second thing that happened made me realise my life was going to change forever.*